Author: Dan Frost

Table of Contents

Prologue:

#1 Victory Royale!

Cobbman13 was so thrilled by the squad's win, that he forgot to be sad for just a moment. It felt good to be on top of the world with such amazing friends, all of whom were celebrating their triumph.

There was Blaze98 with his giant tomato head, who was always the first one to start dancing at the end of the round, laughing with joy. There was GammaRey, in her pristine white body suit, who had been quick to join him. She was always in a good mood when they ranked highly. Then of course, there was Krypto, wiggling around in his familiar Shadow Ops gear. He had been a part of the squad longer than the other two, and Cobb didn't know what things would be like when he left.

Suddenly, he remembered why he had been sad.

They had just played their final round as a squad before Krypto laid down his weapons for good. It had been a great time, but now it was over. Cobb felt like he should say something, being the other founder of their little team. He stopped dancing, hoping to be taken more seriously in the moment, but then finding he had no idea what to say. Luckily, GammaRey stopped moving as well, and beat him to the punch.

"It's not going to be the same without you, Krypto."

Krypto also quit dancing, although Blaze hadn't yet taken the hint and was still flailing around as they began to say their goodbyes.

"I'm going to miss you guys," Krypto said. His tone was more serious than usual, but just as straightforward as ever.

"Are you sure you have to leave?" Gamma asked softly.

"Yeah," Blaze said as he finally stopped his motions. "Who needs to spend more time with their family anyway? We're all the family you need."

That was a surprisingly sincere thing for Blaze to say, and it was at that point Cobb found his voice again, along with the words he'd been searching for. "We need you here, fighting with us."

There was a brief pause before Krypto answered, but he did. "You guys are going to do just fine without me."

Cobbman knew that they probably would be fine, they were all good players, but he also knew that it wouldn't feel right entering the field of battle without Krypto.

"We'll be down a member," Gamma pointed out.

"Our best member, other than me, of course," Blaze said in that joking way he had.

"Our leader," Cobb corrected, before Gamma could get too defensive about it. He didn't want to admit it, but he was feeling very emotional about this whole thing. Playing with the three of them had been one of the best times of his life, and he wasn't ready for it to be behind him.

"I think Cobb should take over as leader," Krypto said coolly, almost as if he had planned to suggest it.

Cobb hadn't been expecting that, and didn't know how to answer.

Blaze on the other hand didn't miss a beat. "I guess it wouldn't be fair for a handsome plant like me to have all these skills and lead the party."

"I'd follow the Cobbman," Gamma said in agreement.

Cobb was honored, sad, nervous, and excited all at once. He felt like it was the best part of the fantasy epic, a hero's rise to greatness. He said the only thing he could think of to say, which was simply, "I accept."

"Well, with that settled, it's time for me to make my exit. You're going to do great, Cobb. And..." Krypto hesitated, obviously feeling somewhat pressured to say something for his final departure. "... it was nice playing with all of you."

They all echoed back that it had been nice playing with him before it was time.

"Goodbye guys, and good luck."

Krypto had signed off.

"We don't need luck, right guys?" Blaze asked once it was just the three of them.

"I certainly don't," Gamma replied.

"I think we'll be okay, if we stick together." Cobb said, trying to sound reassuring while hiding his nerves about his new leadership position.

What he didn't know was that the three of them would need luck, and not just because they were down a member. Somewhere in their little world, a storm was already brewing.

Chapter 1

"Have you guys heard about- "Blaze's voice was drowned out by Gamma yelling at him.

"Pay attention!"

Cobb had been running toward the center of town to try and grab some more supplies while they waited to lure more people toward their fort, but he slowed his pace at that, worried that he might have to come back. "Everything okay?"

"We're fine," Blaze answered.

Gamma didn't seem to agree. "Blaze is going to get us killed. We're still open on one side and he's dancing around, attracting attention."

She'd been a little tense lately. She hoped to one day have a career in the sport, and had made it clear from day one that she was in it to win it. Being down a member put them at a serious disadvantage, and as their squad ranking had slid steadily lower, her mood had been getting worse.

"That's what I always do," Blaze pointed out.

"But it's different now!" Gamma was getting frustrated. "Without Krypto we have to try a lot harder to win."

"You have to relax some."

"And you need to pay attention."

Cobb knew that this was going to be his first real challenge as squad leader. He couldn't have his two people fighting. Gamma had a habit of taking things a little too seriously, but winning was important to her, and Blaze wasn't exactly helping her to calm down any.

Cobb would talk to them both about it to smooth things over before they got worse, but he decided that it could wait until after the round. If he could keep his head down and get a win for the team, Gamma would be in a much better mood and they'd probably both be easier to mediate.

Unfortunately, in trying harder to win, the opposite happened.

As he rushed forward to grab a loot chest, an unseen enemy was able to take him out, shooting him down from nowhere. He realized that their chances of winning had just about gone out the window. "I'm down, guys."

"I can come get you up again," Blaze offered.

Before Cobb could respond to that, he heard Gamma cry out in frustration. "Don't go that way! It's not – "

She barely had time to finish her sentence before the game was lost. Cobb couldn't see what was happening, but he could almost feel the weight of the defeat as they were eliminated.

"Sorry about that," Blaze said. "I thought that alley had been secured." His apology was casual, but Cobb thought it might be a step in the right direction.

"If you had stopped to listen to me, you would have known that it wasn't." Gamma didn't sound like she was in a particularly forgiving mood.

"There wasn't time. Our leader was down."

"There's never time. You're always finding an excuse to go running off and put the group in danger."

There had always been a little bit of friction between Blaze and Gamma, but it had gotten a lot worse since Krypto's departure. Cobb realized there was no time like the present to try and calm them down.

"We have to try and stop fighting," he told them.

9

"But he - "Gamma began to protest, but Cobb remained persistent.

"No, I mean it. Krypto put me in charge, and I'm going to do my best to make sure things keep running smoothly."

"They're not running smoothly," she said. "We haven't won a game for weeks, not since he left."

"It's not about winning all the time," Blaze said. "It's about having fun."

"Winning is fun for me," Gamma said. "-And you make it really hard sometimes."

"Let's not place blame, okay?" Cobb said, determined not to let the arguing start up again. "Blaze takes a lot of risks, yes, but he's been playing like that for a long time. It's going to take awhile to learn how to play with just the three of us, and Gamma, you've been putting a lot of pressure on us to do better. Maybe if you can ease up a little bit, Blaze can try to be a little more careful, and I can try to cover his back a little more."

She sighed. "I'll try. I just hate losing all the time."

"I know, but it will get better." Cobb assured her.

"Maybe it would get better if we had a fourth person?" Blaze asked.

There was a moment of silence before Gamma chimed in. "That would definitely help."

"Oh, right."

Cobb couldn't deny it, the idea made him a little sad. There had been a tiny part of him that had been hoping that Krypto would come back to reclaim his spot, and had wanted to leave it empty. Even though part of him realized that wouldn't be the case, filling the slot would mean giving up on that fantasy altogether.

"We'd probably start winning again if we just had a full squad," Blaze continued.

"And at the very least, being on an even playing field would relieve some of the tension we have going in," Gamma added.

Cobb didn't much like the idea, but he knew that if the other two were agreeing on something, there was not much point in arguing it. Plus, if it was going to keep starting fights between them, he couldn't see the point in delaying a change he knew would have to happen eventually.

"I'll start looking into it."

"We'll need to find someone really good if we want to get back to where we were – the competition has gotten more intense lately."

"That's what I was going to ask you guys about earlier," Blaze said. "Have you noticed that people around here have started getting a lot more competitive the last week or two?"

Cobb couldn't say that he could, but then again, he'd been distracted.

"At first I thought it was just that we weren't doing as well," Gamma said, "but I think maybe you're right."

"It's probably just the end of the season coming up," Cobb said. "But if you're right, we are probably going to need to find that fourth member."

"They need to be someone really good, like Krypto was." Gamma told him.

"Think Slayer is looking to join a squad?" Blaze asked. It was clear from his tone that he was joking, but Cobb was a little scared that it would take the most legendary player to get them back to where they were.

Finding someone good who wasn't already in a squad was going to be difficult, especially in a timely manner. The real challenge, however, was going to be someone who could bridge the gap between Gamma and Blaze's play styles. It wasn't exactly something he could advertise for, and he had no idea how he was going to pull it off.

Chapter 2

The first bad sign was when the new guy didn't say anything. He showed up in a Panda Leader outfit, completely silent. Cobb had asked him several times if he could hear them, but he hadn't gotten back anything resembling a response.

"Maybe it's some kind of technical issue on his end?" Gamma had asked. Maybe it was, but that didn't chance the outcome much one way or the other if they couldn't communicate with their new recruit.

It was exactly the sort of issue that Cobb had been afraid of when they had agreed they'd try just adding a random player in to be the fourth member of their squad. Considering the way things were playing out, he didn't have a good feeling about the upcoming match.

The second bad sign was when, Cobb specifically saying not to, their new guy jumped out of the battle bus and into the middle of Tilted Towers to go chasing the coolest loot. Cobb watched their panda ally get smaller and smaller as he glided down into the chaos.

14

"You have to respect that as a strategy, it takes guts." No one was overly surprised that Blaze admired such a blatant disregard for orders, and even Gamma seemed impressed when he made it out of the initial fight completely unscathed. Cobb had been prepared to meet him halfway to get him back on his feet, but it turned out not to be necessary.

"Great job, Lex," he said. "Now, if you want to meet at the edge of the safe zone, we- "but he didn't get a chance to finish his sentence. Their new member, Lextron, was bashing his way through the streets in the opposite direction from where the three of them were congregated.

"Are we just supposed to follow him around now, or what?" Gamma asked, the irritation clear in her voice. "Because we already have someone like that in the squad, and I didn't sign up for a second one."

Blaze was quick to jump in. "Yeah, everyone gets upset when I jump down early or when I don't follow orders. I don't mind taking risks, but if that's our new plan, I want to be a part of it."

Gamma was taking out her frustration on anything and everything in her way, her pick axe demolishing cars and sides of buildings into piles of raw material.

"Look, it's not a perfect system," he said as he looked at the new guy still smashing away in the distance, "but you guys said that you wanted a fourth, and this was the fastest way to get it done. We were lucky that we just happened to get Lextron. It could have gone a lot worse, he's a good shot."

"He's a great player," Blaze pointed out as they watched him take on another handful of opponents.

"-But he's not a team player," Gamma finished.

There was little denying that.

"Filling the slot isn't the same as finding a fourth member to be a part of the squad," Blaze pointed out as he joined Gamma in collecting some raw resources. "-and you know that."

Cobb did know it, although he found it difficult to take advice from anyone with a tomato for a head. "I know, but..." he was at a loss. He'd been doing his best when he had tried to address the problems of his teammates quickly, and he didn't know what he could do better with such short notice. "Let's just give him a chance though, okay? I mean, he's already with us for the day."

"It might not be so bad, for just today." Gamma agreed.

Cobb was grateful. She came across as harsh, but she was at the very least trying to be open. That had to count for something.

"You're just saying that because of his building skills," Blaze teased.

Gamma stopped what she was doing to turn and look in the direction that Lextron had taken off. He was building a ramp up to the sky, a technique that was far from uncommon, but also one that usually wasn't pulled out while there were so many opponents left in the field.

"Lex, are you sure you want to be doing that?" Cobb asked.

Of course, there was no response.

"We'd better go get him," Gamma said after a moment.

None of them were thrilled to be rushing over there, but they all went because for the time being, Lex was part of their team. Cobb thought it was nice to have the three of them working for a common goal again as well.

Of course, the lack of planning had put them at a real disadvantage, and they had all lost quite a bit of health by the time they had made it up to the base of the ramp, where they were greeted by more enemies.

To his credit, Lextron performed very well. Whatever great weapon he'd been able to snag by jumping out of the bus first was helping him thin out all of the enemies swarming around them, but his recklessness had left him exposed and outnumbered.

They tried to make it up to him, but they were just too late. The round was lost.

"If he does the same thing next time, at least we'll be able to prepare," Blaze pointed out, looking on the bright side of the situation.

"That's true. We'll have to work around him a little better next time, but it's not that different from our usual strategy."

"I'll jump in early to grab a good gun and watch his back, you and Gamma can get supplies wherever, and we'll follow him closely next time. You guys can set up a base around the ramp and I can fight whoever comes over there."

"It's not the worst idea I've ever heard, but he's already gone," Gamma pointed out.

It was true. While Cobb and Blaze had been trying to make a strategy around Lex, he had made his departure from their presence without ever saying a single word.

"Alright," Cobb said, scrambling to adapt to yet another curve ball being thrown at him. "Well, we can get another random person in for the rest of today, and who knows? Maybe one of them will work out better."

"Maybe," Gamma said, but he could hear the hesitation in her voice.

"Playing with random people was how Krypto found you, Gamma," Cobb pointed out.

"Although, I'm still not completely sold on his decision to add you permanently," Blaze said, chuckling a bit at his own joke.

"I was here before you!" she shot back, but Cobb could tell that she wasn't too angry, and Blaze just started laughing louder. When it died down she turned her attention back to the matter at hand. "I'll follow you, Cobb, if you decide this is best. But... finding another random player who might not get along with us, or who might not be any good, it feels a lot like starting over."

Cobb understood exactly what she meant.

Chapter 3

Blaze98 was back.

The second that the battle bus was over land he was jumping, right into the thick of it all, feeling like himself for the first time in a while. Other people were landing all around him, guns were blazing, and he could feel his adrenaline pumping. This was action. This was where the best part of the fight was, big stakes for a big payoff – just the way he liked it. This was something that his squad didn't encourage, something he had forgotten all about in his complacency.

In a weird way, the failure with Lextron had really inspired him.

Despite what his friends might say about his reckless manner of jumping into things, it worked, and that strategy had gotten them further in a group than any of Gamma's caution or fort-building.

Ahead of him, barred by only a handful of other ambitious players, was a loot chest. In it, he could almost feel the promise of a rare weapon.

It would feel so good to be able to claim something valuable for himself first thing instead of scrambling around with gray guns until they could snipe someone with something better near the base. That had never been his favorite method of attaining things, though he'd have had to admit, it was satisfying in its own way.

He landed next to another player, much closer than intended and before he knew what had hit him he had taken his first blow from their axe. He dodged the second blow easily, knowing that it would be better to find a firearm to defend himself with than to try and fight back with his own axe – especially since he'd be getting the second hit in.

Unfortunately, someone else had had the same idea as him.

They had dropped down after him, but only by a second, and they had landed closer to the box. Blaze was sure he could make it though, he was determined, and he had the edge.

Until he took another hit.

With 20% of his health gone he instinctively turned back to look at his attacker as he kept moving forward. That distraction was just enough to bring him down, as his opponent got the loot before he did. Sure enough, there was a blue gun inside and no sooner had he dodged another pick axe blow from behind him than he had been shot several times by the faster man.

Even a full minute after he had fallen, couldn't believe what had just happened. It was one thing to be able to laugh at himself when he messed up, but there hadn't been anything funny or exciting about just getting distracted and not doing well.

When he had first started entering the rounds, he had used make or break strategies all the time, and had almost always made it past that initial scramble to safety – even if he hadn't always been the last man-standing. He'd always gotten a higher kill count, for sure, had always been able to hold his head high after.

What had just happened was something that he could only describe as a terrible failure on his part. Maybe he was just rusty. He tried to tell himself that's what it was. He had gotten used to someone covering him, and it would take him a few rounds to readjust to being on his own.

When Cobb had suggested that they all work on some of their individual skillsets while he searched for a new member, Blaze had taken to the idea very well. He knew that he was at the top of his game already, he always was, and with the even ground provided to him in a solo match he'd been sure that he'd come out on top. He'd even considered not going back to the squad if it went well enough. After all, there had been a time when he had preferred that, not so long ago.

Whether it was because he was losing, or perhaps because there was no one there with him to share the pain of his loss, he realized that he missed his squad. It was nice to have someone to complain to when things went badly, and he realized, more rewarding to have people there to share in his victories. He liked having the others there with him, and suddenly he found that he was once more invested in whether or not Cobb would find someone.

He promised himself two things before boarding the next bus. The first was that he would keep practicing until he heard from the others, so that they would never find out how miserably he had done on his own. The second was that, if given the chance, he would do whatever it took to make sure that the squad stayed together.

Chapter 4

GammaRey was feeling good about her chances at taking the victory. She had holed herself up in a fort that was some of her finest work. It was so much easier to build without Blaze drawing attention to her location or Cobb telling her to cover someone. Her mind for strategy was so much better utilized when she was given the room that she needed to shine. Things were going great for a change.

The way that she had built things up, her base built off the side of one of the abandoned houses, in an alley where she'd been able to scavenge plenty of supplies, and still a decent way from the edge of the safe zone, where another storm threatened to close in. With any luck, she'd be able to wait out the last of the stragglers that made it that close to the center of the field. The house itself was in good enough shape that it might be a tempting location to look for loot – loot which she had already taken, of course.

She'd been using a green gun taken from the home in the earlier part of the round, before she'd been able to score herself a blue version of it from someone she had sniped after first setting up shop there in the alley.

It was a good system, and she was careful.

With the tactical edge, all she had to do was just to wait it out, look for any opportune times to attack, and make the most of her hard-earned advantages.

Something had been lost, though.

Certainly nothing practical, as she was more than confident in her ability to hold her position by herself, but part of the experience that maybe not even victory could replace. Another two minutes passed and there was little denying that there was something to be said for not playing it safe all the time. As more players dropped off and her chances got better and better, the excitement ebbed away more and more.

A player ran out into her field of vision and she got him with a handful of precise shots. Above him, as his weapons dropped, she could see a purple glow from where he had fallen.

It was tempting. A weapon that rare would undoubtedly give her the edge as it got down to the last group of fighters. She knew that Blaze wouldn't hesitate to run out there and grab it, but that was the same sort of insane, hands-on approach that always got them into trouble. Besides, she wasn't playing in a squad anymore, so there was no one to help her if she got caught trying something too ambitious.

Plus, she reasoned, a purple item was a good lure if she wanted to continue sniping people without drawing a lot of unnecessary attention to herself by building up, as would be the more common approach.

As the numbers dwindled down to four, then three, and then at last two, she still hadn't picked up the gun. The eye of the storm was getting smaller and smaller, and at long last she was able to bring down the final opponent.

1 *Victory Royale.*

She had known that was coming, but it still tasted a sweet. A carefully planned win was still a win and although the wait to get there had been long, it had been worth it. There was a difference, she reminded herself, between cowardice and precision, and she knew that not taking that epic weapon had won her the game. She patted herself on the back for her restraint, and taking a leaf out of Blaze's book, she allowed herself a victory dance.

She felt lighter, and in a better mood than she had been for a while. Wins always cheered her up. She wondered if she played a couple solo rounds on her own, even once the squad back together, if that would be enough to tide her over until they figured out how to get back to the top of their game. That way she could spend some time with her friends, but she'd have some time to herself as well, to take things seriously and score herself some wins. It felt so good to be the last one standing for a change.

Her joy was short lived however, as she noticed a strange announcement being made.

The biggest storm is coming.

That was strange. She hadn't seen anything like that follow up a victory announcement before.

Chapter 5

Entering into the battles had just been a distraction. Cobbman hadn't been able to realize that at the time, but it seemed obvious now that it was just him, and he had been given some time to think. Fighting for victory in the midst of a storm had been an exciting break from the woes of everything else. The feel of the weapon in his hands, the thrill of facing off against players that were as good or better than him, it had all been a way to escape. It had been something that he could lose himself in when he was feeling down.

Now, as he jumped from the battle bus and opened his parachute, looking for a place to land, he realized he had gotten too carried away with the fantasy of the whole thing. He was stressing himself out trying to make things better than they were so that it could all live up to his high expectations.

In that period of his life just before he had started Battle Royale, he'd been a big fan of stories. All of his favorite involved groups of heroes or adventurers, underdogs who banded together to live exciting lives and grow closer together. He'd had that for a short amount of time, back when he'd been playing with Krypto, and it had seemed like their little squad was meant for great things, having a good time along the way. It had felt like everything he'd wanted, but if the squad couldn't survive losing a single member, then maybe they weren't as close as he had thought.

He had been happy to accept the role as leader when his friend had suggested it, and in the moment he had seen it as a great call to action that would kick off the next phase of their adventures together, but now he wasn't sure he was cut out for it. It felt like he was having to try too hard to keep the peace among everyone, and he hadn't been able to accomplish the one real leadership task they had given him; to find a new member.

He was in the top five, and it didn't surprise him when he didn't make it any further than that – not in that round, and not in any of the other rounds he plated that night. He was too stubborn to quit, and too distracted to do well. His mind was on what he would tell the others the next day when they got together.

They would probably be expecting him to show up with another player, but he hadn't made any progress on that. The last week he'd been joining random squads, trying to find someone looking for a group, and had turned up no one. He'd sent out some feelers in the forums and although there had been a few leads, he hadn't gotten a definite answer from anyone.

While he was wondering how his friends were faring on their own, he lost another round.

"What am I going to do?" He asked as he watched the storm shrink over his body. He hadn't even been paying attention to where he was going. He decided to call it quits for the night, assuring himself that things would be better in the morning.

Chapter 6

"So, how did everyone's solo adventures go?" Cobb asked, although he rather suspected that he knew. The squad might be more important to him than it was to the others, but he couldn't imagine that they would have been waiting for them if they didn't want to be back.

"I won a few rounds," Gamma said casually, as though it didn't mean much to her one way or the other. Cobb was encouraged by her light tone, and hoped that the wins would get her in a better mindset for the fight they'd be heading into.

"I'm not surprised," Blaze commented. He seemed to be in a cheery enough mood as well, although he was suspiciously quiet about his own victories, or lack thereof.

"I did," she said. "I had almost forgotten what it felt like. Hopefully we can do a little of that today?"

Cobb smiled to himself, happy that she seemed to be taking that positive energy and applying it to their goals as a team.

"I say we do it!" Blaze said.

"I'm liking this energy, guys." Cobbman told them. "So let's stick to our usual strategy. Gamma, since you're on a hot streak, do you think you can work alone while I cover Blaze?"

"So, no new member then?"

He had gotten so excited by the mood of his friends that he had almost forgotten he had bad news for them, which was in this instance, no news at all. He sighed. "Well, I thought I found someone who looked pretty promising. He had experience playing in a squad, and was easy enough to get along with from what little I talked to him. I thought today might be a good chance to see how he fit in..."

"But...?" Gamma prompted him as his words started to slow and he tried to stall.

"But, he didn't show up, I guess. He said he might be here, but I haven't heard anything from him all day."

"So looking in the forums was a bust, is what you're saying?" Blaze asked.

He had gotten through the worst of it, and now it

was time to just power through and get them to the battle bus. "I was hoping to have someone today, but I promise you guys, I haven't given up on finding us a fourth. The forums gave me some good leads, it's just that none of them have panned out yet. Eventually, one of them will, and in the meantime, there's nothing stopping us from improving our game."

There was a moment of silence where he wasn't sure that his pep talk had worked, before Gamma eventually broke it. "What are we going to do for today, though?"

Cobb thought it might be best for the three of them to go back to just being short a person, so as not to add any more tension to their group like they had when playing with Lextron, but he didn't feel confident enough to decide for everyone.

"Let's put it to a vote," he said. "We can either put in a random fourth like we did with Lex, or we can hang tight with just the three of us, try to improve our game before finding a permanent fourth."

"If we get good enough waiting, maybe we don't have to find a permanent fourth," Blaze pointed out. Cobb hadn't wanted to say it, but he'd been hoping for the same thing.

"The idea of strengthening our game with just the three of us makes some sense," Gamma said, putting that analytical brain to work. "Although, we might just stumble across a good fit if we keep filling the slot with random people."

"It would be nice if our problem just happened to resolve itself," Blaze agreed, and for a moment Cobb thought he might be outvoted.

He couldn't help but weigh in a little. "Well, I don't mind finding a fill in that way, although the chances of finding someone randomly who we get along with and meets everyone's standards is not great, to say the least."

"And," Blaze added, now arguing his own points. "I really don't like the idea of playing with someone who is just going to end up calling the shots because they ignore us, like last time."

"It's funny that you should be the one to have a problem with that, Blaze." Gamma pointed out quietly.

Cobb stepped in before the two of them could get lost in any of their usual, competitive banter. "We don't have a lot of time before we board the battle bus, so what's everyone thinking?"

"I vote we find another player." Gamma said.

"I vote just the three of us," Blaze said, to which Gamma sighed audibly.

"I think I'm going to side with Blaze this time," Cobb said with some relief. It wasn't as good as the vote being unanimous, but he was happy that it had gone his way. He didn't want to have to worry about a new person for at least one day. "That might be the best way to see how far we came while we were all practicing on our own."

They'd decided just in time, it would seem, as it was time for them all to board the bus.

The storm will be starting in two minutes.

"Oh, right!" Gamma sounded almost surprised by the announcement, which they'd heard together so often.

"Is everything okay?" Cobb asked her.

"I just remembered something. I was going to ask you guys- "

But their attention was immediately caught by Blaze, who had already jumped out of the bus.

"I should probably go after him," Cobb said.

"Right," Gamma agreed. "We don't want to lose this early in the round. We'll talk about it later."

Later came a lot sooner than any of them wanted, as it turned out to be their worst round yet.

As Cobb rushed forward to help find some good cover for Blaze, Blaze doubled back, rounding the corner and finding himself with a weapon pointed right in his face. He was down, and Cobb suddenly found himself caught between two enemies who were both shooting at him.

All he was able to do was to try and drink a potion as he ducked behind a wall that was being constructed, but he knew that it wouldn't be enough. "Gamma, we need –" but before the words were out, he was down.

It wasn't even a full minute later that she had also fallen.

"I guess we didn't get better at all," she said bitterly.

Cobb was disheartened. She'd seemed like she was in a better mood, they all had. He'd thought that the round would go a lot better than it had. "I was just thrown when Blaze tried to double back, it was an accident. It happens all the time, it happened all the time when Krypto was here."

"Not all the time," Gamma pointed out. "We won sometimes when Krypto was here."

It hurt, but that didn't make it any less true. "Listen, it was just a bad round. It happens."

"Yeah," Blaze said. "Now, what did you want to ask us?"

"If you had listened to me at the beginning of the round, instead of cutting me off, maybe we'd still be in the running," she pointed out.

"Gamma-" Cobb started.

"No, she's right." Blaze said. "I was just trying to get a jump on the round. I wanted us to do well, that's all."

Gamma paused. "I'm sorry too. I thought that because I was doing so well on my own, I'd be able to take this a little less seriously, but I just, I hate losing all the time. I especially hate losses like this, where we weren't even close."

37

"When we find a fourth, things will get better," Cobb assured her.

"If we ever do," she said. "And until we do, I think maybe I need some time to go back to playing alone. This whole situation has been really tense, and it would probably be better for me to get some space."

"Wait-" Cobb called after her, but she had already logged off. Feeling a little panicked, he turned to his friend. "She'll be back, right? Things will be better when we have a full squad again.

"Totally," Blaze said, although he wasn't entirely convincing.

"Yeah?"

"Yeah, I mean, probably." He hesitated. "She has a point though, I think, about maybe needing some space. In the meantime, or... it might be easier to just move on at this point, you know?"

Cobb was crushed. It wasn't a good feeling realizing that he might have just lost something so important to him. "I see."

The silence between them felt so awkward. "I'll see you around though, yeah?"

"Yeah," he said, and just like that he was all alone, uncertain if that was the last time he'd see his squad mates.

Chapter 7

Cobbman13 felt weirdly guilty about tagging up with a stranger. Finding someone to enter the Battle Royale with was the whole problem that he was having with his squad, so hitting a button to assign someone to him felt almost wrong – even if it was just a Duo match instead of Squad. On the other hand, he knew that he was more adaptable, and it would be easy for him to be matched up with someone for a round – not to mention that it felt a lot better than playing alone.

He was paired up with a stranger, of course, with the name of Zombie Ace.

She was wearing a skin he'd never come across before, a shiny gray and black outfit with an asymmetrical cut and a hood covering her face. He thought the presumed rarity of her attire was a good design because it meant she was probably someone who wasn't just there casually. This was confirmed when she got straight to business. "I like to go in with a game plan."

He liked that, and it felt nice not to have to be the one to try and make people focus. He almost told her that he wanted to go in for a safe strategy, the kind that he was used to pitching to his squad, but he felt uncomfortable stepping into the role of leader with a complete stranger. Even though he had experience coming up with plans and giving orders, it hadn't exactly been going the best for him.

"Well, I'm open. How do you like to play?"

"I'm used to doing this solo, so I'm not great at playing support. I'd like to jump down early; have you watch my back. Is that cool?"

He had experience with that too. It wasn't his favorite thing in the world, and he didn't think it made their chances of winning much higher than just winging it, but at least she was upfront about the whole thing. If things went disastrously, he could find a new partner at the end of the round, which was more or less what he expected would happen anyway. He was rapidly adjusting to the idea that his allies in the battle would just continue to come and go, until he eventually decided he didn't have to sign back in. So he agreed to her strategy without much thought. "That's cool."

"Great."

It was about time for them to get on the battle bus, which was ideal because he wasn't sure what to say and she didn't seem to be the type for making conversation.

For as easy as their strategy was to follow, they probably should have talked about it more, which he realized almost immediately. When she said that she wanted to jump early, she meant it. The first storm announcement had barely passed before she had her parachute out and was sailing for the land mass below. He scrambled to follow, pulling out his pick axe as he prepared for a rough landing.

He knew that there would be a lot of people touching the ground there, and the building that she going in for looked like it would be very crowded. He did his best to follow her while aiming for the edge of the building, not wanting to get caught right in between enemies. He was playing support after all, and he couldn't make sure that his partner was alive if he was dead.

She was the first one down.

Several other players rushed toward her, axes

raised, but she had the jump on them and was the first one to touch a gun. In sheer numbers they could probably have taken her down, but he was quick to move in as soon as he landed, chopping and swinging away at everyone frantically so that they had to focus more on dodging than on killing.

"I've got them, grab a weapon."

There were plenty of loot boxes in the building just underneath them, and he got a decent a number of supplies as he tore his way through the first few barriers before finding a nice, blue weapon for himself. It was a little more precision based than what he usually went for, but it was enough to take out the stragglers who had followed after him.

There weren't many of them.

Perhaps it was just luck that let her survive, but he didn't think so. As she came to meet him, the last one standing from the initial battle, he realized that this was something she had done many, many times before. It was more skill than anything, and she had known all along that her risky move would pay off, making the stunt far less risky than if someone like Blaze98 had tried it just to show off or "because he felt like it."

They exited through the back of the building together, tearing out one of the walls and rushing down the street, collecting building materials as they went.

He had thought that covering her would be like covering Blaze usually was, where he was just cleaning up mess after mess until he got himself killed in the process, but it turned out to be a lot more cautious than that. Her moves were calculated, her shots precise, and the only time she slowed was before peering around corners. He was actually somewhat reminded of how Krypto used to play. It wasn't often that he came across someone who was as unarguably talented as his friend had been.

As the others in the arena fought amongst themselves, she set about collecting more resources from the ravaged cityscape around them. He followed her direction, but not silently as it seemed she might have preferred. He was getting an idea, and thought it couldn't hurt to test the waters.

"You said you don't play with partners very often?" He asked her.

"No, I prefer solo games."

"So why the shift?" He tried not to sound too eager, and not to get his hopes up.

"I keep hearing about this storm that's coming," she answered simply.

"There are storms coming all the time."

"It's not like that. This one is supposed to be different."

"Different how?" He wasn't sure he liked the sound of that. He remembered the message he had seen the other day about the big storm that was supposed to be coming, after the victory had already been announced. He wondered if that was what she was talking about.

"It's hard to say, no one really knows for sure. But there are rumors. Something's up, and I've heard that partnering up might be the safest way to go for now."

"What about squads?" He had meant to ease into that topic a little more, but the eerie conversation about the bigger storm had distracted him, and people were going down fast. He thought it might be a good idea to get to the heart of it.

She snorted a bit. "What about them? Have you

tried getting into a random squad? Especially lately, no one knows what they're doing."

That was all too true. He thought about asking her right then if she wanted to join, but he hesitated. His friends hadn't exactly parted on the best terms and he wasn't sure if he'd have a squad to invite her to, even if she would agree to do it.

"There are some good ones though, I was in one once."

"Once?" She asked, but then her attention was pulled from the sound of shots fired nearby. "Follow me," she said, darting around behind one of the buildings that she hadn't yet destroyed.

He complied, rushing to in to watch her back. "Right behind you."

She didn't bring the conversation back around until they'd made it a safe distance and she'd scoped out the surrounding area. "So what happened?"

"Well, one of our members had to quit. It all fell to pieces after that, no one liked the disadvantage of only having three people. It was too hard to replace him."

She saw right through him. "Are you asking me to join?"

"Well, I," he turned around when he heard someone approaching from behind and shot them. "He probably had a partner around here somewhere."

"Stay here." Zombie doubled back around to see if she could find their partner, who was racing forward to res their fallen ally. She got them while Cobb held their position. She rejoined him shortly. "You were saying?"

"I was just saying that we had pretty much given up on the idea of having a whole team, but this was only recently. If you were interested-" he was cut off again as she began shooting at someone just around the corner.

 # 1Victory Royale.

For a second he was afraid she would vanish now that they had won, and he'd be left with nothing but a fading sense of hope, but she actually answered the question that he still hadn't managed to get out.

"I could be talked into giving it a go. Just once, to

see if it works out."

"I'll see if I can get everyone together again, I can send you the information."

"Good, do that. I wouldn't normally, and this isn't a permanent arrangement, mind you. It's just something until whatever this weird thing is passes." There was a moment of silence.

The biggest storm is almost here.

"You might want to get them together soon if you want to try this," she added before she signed off. "I think things are about to change around here."

Chapter 8

"Are you sure they're going to show up?" Zombie asked him. It was obvious by the anxious way she was moving around the lobby that she wasn't accustomed to waiting on people, and Cobb couldn't blame her. He couldn't remember the last time he'd had to wait so long for his squad.

"I'm sure," he answered. He hoped that they wouldn't let him down.

"What are they like?"

He was relieved to find that he was spared from answering by Blaze, who had entered the lobby. "Better late than never, right?" He asked, in way of greeting.

Cobb was relieved to see that Blaze had turned up, although he was a bit surprised that Gamma was the last to join them. She was usually the most punctual out of any of them, but then again, she hadn't yet responded to any of his messages. There was a chance that she might not show at all. Cobb tried not to think about it, and turned his attention back to Zombie, answering her question.

"Why don't you meet them for yourself? Zombie, this is Blaze, Blaze, this is Zombie."

"Were you telling the new girl all about me?"

"She was just asking what you and Gamma are like."

"Well, I'm Blaze, I'm the talent."

Cobb wasn't sure how true that was, or what Gamma might think if he was there. They had never really seen Blaze as the talent, so much as the comic relief, although there was something entertaining about his consistent confidence. He decided not to say anything about it though. Zombie played like a pro, and she could probably tell all she needed to know about Blaze from his tomato suit. This was as good as confirmed by her silence, which Blaze seemed to take in stride.

"Have you heard from Gamma?"

"Not yet," Cobb admitted.

"You think she'll show?"

She did, but only at the last minute, when he had practically resigned himself to the fact that they'd be short a member anyway, and the whole thing would be a giant mess. He had never been so relieved to see her sleek, white body suit walk through that door.

"I'm glad you could join us, Gamma."

"Well, I heard you finally found us a fourth, and things have been getting sort of crazy out there."

"Gamma, this is Zombie, our fourth."

"A pleasure to meet you," Gamma said, and she sounded sincere. "It's nice to finally have another girl around here."

"It's good to be here. Like you said, it's been getting pretty crazy out there for anyone playing alone."

They were quickly running out of time, and even though Cobb was glad to see everyone getting along, he knew they'd have to work out a strategy quick.

"So Zombie, what we used to do is have two people drop down early,"

"The sooner the better," Blaze added.

Cobb continued "-and then two of us would establish a base somewhere a little safer."

"I'd be willing to drop down early," Zombie said, just as Cobb had expected.

"And you know that's how I prefer to do things," Blaze added quickly.

"Looks like it's you and I will fort-building again Gamma, if that works for you?"

"Works for me." No sooner had she agreed than it was time to board the bus.

Storm will be approaching in two minutes.

The familiar words were more terrifying to him in that instant than they had been since his first time entering the Battle Royale. There was a part of him that needed for things to go well, and it was so easy for him to see ways in which it might not.

He half expected Zombie and Blaze to go to war with one another for who could be the quickest to drop, but she displayed more patience than he had expected. When Blaze opened his parachute, she followed suit and Cobb felt more confident helping Gamma when he knew that there were two risk takers jumping into immediate combat who would be able to watch each other's backs.

"We should start gathering supplies here in a minute, when it's safe to jump off." He told her.

He could almost hear Gamma's smile as she spoke. "You know I'm not going to argue with that. You think they're going to be okay?"

"I think so." He hoped more than thought, but somehow, miraculously, he was right.

They dropped down near the outskirts of the little city, and Cobbman was pleased with the haul that they were able to take in. He got his shields up and a decent amount of building material as Gamma started seeking for an ideal spot to hunker down in.

"We might have to get a little closer to the center, it doesn't make a lot of sense to camp here if the storm's just going to close in any minute anyway."

"We'll meet you in the middle," Blaze said over the mic and Cobb could tell from the sound of his voice that he seemed pleased with whatever weapons he'd been able to acquire.

"We're East of you guys," Gamma informed them after briefly consulting her map.

"Got it," Zombie confirmed.

Already the fighting amongst squad members seemed to be to a minimum and he was getting back that feeling of working with a group — a feeling he had sorely missed.

On the way there he found a decent gun, after which point he dropped behind Gamma to cover her while she looked for a good location. She found one in a thin alley that provided good cover. "It would keep us from running in an ambush, but if we get a sniper up on one of the adjacent buildings, we'll be able to see any attacks coming."

"On it," Zombie said as she rounded the corner, entering the building to work her way up from the inside while doing a quick sweep of the interior for supplies. Cobbman could see even in passing that she seemed to be geared up fittingly for the upcoming battle. Blaze too was wielding one of his favorite guns.

"It looks like you guys did pretty well," he applauded his returned cohorts.

"No one was a match for the two of us," Blaze replied with satisfaction.

Someone was a match for their group, however, at least as far as hiding was concerned. There was little denying it. The eye of the storm shrank with only one other squad remaining, and they were nowhere to be seen.

"I can go searching for them," Blaze offered.

"We have a good vantage point here," Gamma insisted. "It's better for us to wait them out."

They eye shrank again before Zombie chimed in. "I see them, they're starting to build a ramp."

It seemed that the other surviving squad seemed to have a similar plan to them, and were a little bit faster to begin executing it. "Alright, well we can build faster. Cobbman, help me."

Gamma was on it, and there was little arguing with her ramping skills. She built quickly and with confidence, and her framework in the alley gave them the edge, even though they were the second to start.

"Wait, hold on. There's only one of them building."

No sooner had Zombie said that than the other

three members of the squad came rounding the corner to the alley, charging at them full force. Blaze was still on the ground and outnumbered considerably. Zombie was quick to bring down the enemies' health from her position on the room, and they began to slow their attack considerably.

Blaze had already fallen by the time Cobbman made it back to the ground but Gamma and Zombie both had his back, so they outnumbered the remaining squad by three to two.

Before he knew that the fight had really started, it was over and he was rewarded with the phrase that he'd been hoping for.

 # 1Victory Royale.

He knew without discussion that he had saved his squad, not just in the one fight, but for the future. The feeling was short lived as their victory announcement was replaced by the ominous words:

The biggest storm is arriving now.

"Well that's new," Gamma said anxiously.

"I guess it's a good thing we finally found a fourth," Blaze said through his nervous chuckle.

There was no humor in Zombie's voice when she answered him, however. "Yeah, it looks like you guys are really going to need me."

Chapter 9

Even in the lobby it was clear that what they were going into was not like anything they had faced before, either together or by themselves. The lobby was filled with other recent royale victors, all of whom looked as confused and anxious about what was happening. There were no victory dances, and everyone was huddled up in their groups of four.

"Is this some sort of glitch?" Zombie asked,

"Or a special event, maybe?" Blaze suggested.

"I think it must have something to do with those weird messages that started showing up at the end of the games." Gamma said, with more conviction than the other two had been able to manage.

"Yeah," Cobb added. "I remember, you were going to tell us about that before, well, before we almost split up."

"Are you talking about those impending storm warnings that have been showing up after rounds?" Zombie asked.

"Yeah, I saw a lot of them while I was doing solo rounds, they only seem to show up after victories."

"If that were the case, I probably would have noticed them more," Blaze said, but his comment was ignored by the group.

"A group of winners competing against each other in a storm bigger than what we've seen?" Cobb asked, trying to figure out how and why something like that would be arranged. "That seems strange."

"You'd think that it would be optional, at least." Gamma pointed out. That was the most unsettling part, he had to admit, that they had all just been brought right to the lobby.

"Maybe it's just that exclusive," Blaze said hopefully. "If it is only for winners, it makes sense that they might want to keep it a secret."

"Yeah, but shouldn't there be some sort of opt out or, you know, warning?" Gamma asked.

Cobb had to agree with her. There was something off about the whole event, and he knew that it was going to be intense. "Well, unless anyone feels like trying to opt out now or find whoever's in charge to complain to, we should probably just try to work out a strategy."

"Winging it worked pretty well for us last time," Blaze said. "We came up with a plan with less than a minute to go, and there was no problem."

"We're going to be up against some of the best, though," Zombie argued "Going in unprepared might not be in our best interest this time around."

Gamma was quick to agree. "And for as much as I like strategies that are dependent on my building skills, I'm not sure that's the way to go when we're playing on this kind of level. A lot of players are going to be expecting that this time around and will have made their plans around at least one squad doing that. The last thing we want is to be predictable."

"So what do we do instead?" Blaze asked. "I feel confident just running in, guns blazing."

"We don't have guns to go in blazing with." Gamma pointed out.

"Yes, we do." Zombie's voice was soft, and Cobbman almost missed it. Even once it registered it took him a moment to realize she was right.

"We got to carry guns over from the last round." He said in surprise as he realized that he still held his weapon.

"Well that's great!" Blaze said. "Even more reason to go in with my plan."

"Has that ever happened before?" Gamma asked.

"Not that I've ever heard of." Cobbman answered. "Blaze, Ace, have you ever seen anything like this?"

They both responded in the negative.

"Well whether this is a glitch or an event or.... whatever else this is going to be, I think it's safe to assume that it's going to be dangerous."

They weren't given much more time to discuss strategy, as it was time to board the bus.

The biggest storm is approaching in two minutes.

Cobb tried to take stock of how the other teams were doing for weapons, and while their squad wasn't the worst off, they didn't seem to be the best off either. That made him nervous, as did the sky.

Everything, the clouds and the landing zone alike,

were cast in a deep shade of purple - the scary shade that he had learned through countless tournaments to associate with death and poison. This was going to be a storm unlike anything they'd seen before, and he knew his squad would be looking to him to get them all through it.

"Guys," he started. It was time for him to make a call and get a strategy together. "I want to wait to the last minute to drop. Since we have weapons it would be smarter to get to safety and avoid the crowd as much as possible until it thins out. This is unknown territory, and if there was ever a time to play it safe, that time would be now."

No sooner had his fellow squad mates agreed than a cloud intercepted the path of the battle bus which shook several individuals free. If he hadn't already been so full of dread, seeing that would have done it.

With people scrambling and panicking and all his plans out the window, he knew that it was time for them to jump, even if they lost the other minute and a half they'd been planning on having for strategizing.

"Now!" He cried before the clouds got any closer. Gamma had been knocked close to the edge and he could see Zombie already reaching for her parachute. Blaze was nowhere to be seen in the confusion.

Whatever this new, bigger storm was, it was upon them.

Chapter 10

Even as he approached the ground, Cobbman13 knew that he would be in for a rough landing. The 'approaching' storm was all around him, the winds blowing him violently off course and dangerously close to being outside of the safe zone. He could feel his health draining more than once as he breathed in the poison he was being guided into.

The only thing he was able to take comfort from was that everyone seemed to be having trouble landing, not just him. He could also see that Zombie and Gamma had landed close to one another. Blaze98 was still nowhere to be seen – and with his ridiculous costume on, he should have been the easiest to spot from just about anywhere on the field.

"Blaze?" He called as he finally dropped down to the earth.

"I landed outside the drop zone."

Cobb was panicked hearing that. He had never seen anyone die from poison so early in a round, and he didn't want to start now, especially when the person in danger was one of his own squad mates.

"Are you safe? Can you find the circle?"

"I'm in it now, but it's shrinking really quickly."

"Shrinking?" He demanded. They had only just landed, and barely been able to achieve that. There was no way that the storm could already be shrinking. Blaze came rushing up from the left, however, Cobb could see that the wall of the storm was steadily closing in behind him. It was like nothing he had ever seen before.

"Quick, get what you can and run!" He ordered, but he could see that there was a flaw in that as well.

Aside from the few stranded vehicles that Gamma and Zombie had already started demolishing, there was little in the way of resources. They hadn't landed in the middle or even in the outskirts of a city, but out in the open. There were no buildings they could re-purpose, no loot boxes, nothing to hide behind — it was all flat, dirty plains in that unsettling shade of violet.

In the distance he could see the other side of the

storm closing in as well, and in the center was just a handful of competitors. He could see virtually the entire area of battle there from their position at the edge, and even though there were far fewer people in the arena than had boarded the bus, he knew that it was going to be a fierce fight. He also knew it would be more about surviving the storm than the others.

"What's our plan here, boss?" Gamma asked.

"And no pressure, but we need an answer pretty fast," Zombie added.

As if to add more pressure, there was an announcement.

The Biggest storm is closing in.

"We can see that," Blaze said under his breath.

"Stay toward the edge of safe zone, don't go rushing in until we need to, but go about it safely. Blaze, let me help you."

He turned over his shield potions and what little bit of health restoratives he had to Blaze, who was still at less than half health when all was said and done, and it was time to start moving again.

"I don't have the supplies to build much for a fort," Gamma informed them as they began to cautiously move forward.

Cobb wasn't sure what sort of fort would be able to help them in this place anyway. "Just press forward as best you can."

All their supplies were limited. They couldn't just go shooting blindly. Considering that he couldn't see any materials, guns, or potions, he didn't think they'd be able to pick up much ammo either.

"If I were in the center," Zombie pointed out. "I wouldn't wait for everyone to slowly come to me as I picked them off one by one. I would-"

"Try to rush them when the crowds got thin enough?" Gamma asked, watching as the few remaining squads slowly continued to approach one another.

"Exactly. You either push them into the storm or gun them down, and they don't stand a chance."

They were steadily approaching that point as shots began firing ahead of them.

"So what you're saying, is the squad that landed

67

closest to the center of the field has as good as won the match?" Cobb asked in frustration. That's where Zombie seemed to be headed with her explanation, and he could tell that Gamma was having similar thoughts.

"Not necessarily," Blaze said and before anyone could stop him he had rushed toward the center of the group with no regard for safety of any sort.

It was the kind of reckless, insane tactic that never should have been attempted – especially by someone with so little health. It was one for the playbooks, an insane stunt that only worked in the sort of stories that Cobb had so much appreciation for, the kind of stories that had made him accept the role of leader in the first place.

Blaze knew what he was getting into when he made the move, knew that Cobb or any of the others wouldn't be able to resurrect him once he went charging in, but he did it anyway. And on some slim, slim chance, it worked. Immediately all of the fire was directed toward the center of the field, toward the lunatic charging in. Logic dictated that he should have fallen in a second but miraculously, a lot of the fire took out the squad that he had charged to – the squad with the vantage point he had wanted. He was even able to pick up one of their weapons before he fell.

The three of them made the most of his distraction. Cobb went around the left perimeter of the storm, Gamma went around the right, and they charged forward, guns blazing as their ally had wanted while Zombie rushed up to where he had fallen to secure the center of the safe zone.

For a moment Cobb didn't focus on what the others were doing. He was charging into danger, and it was exhilarating. He was absorbing shots and taking damage, but he knew that he had to go forward fearlessly, and so he did. When he saw that he had a clear path to Gamma, he knew that they had won.

To his relief, the storm stopped moving and the announcement was made.

 # 1Victory Royale.

The words had never seemed so sweet, and as he knelt down to resurrect Blaze, he wondered what would become of them, now that the biggest storm had been conquered.

Epilogue:

"That was the best thing we've ever done!" Blaze couldn't have been happier in the lobby. Cobb could remember a time when he'd always been bitter not to be standing at the end of a round, but the excitement of the whole thing seemed to have gotten him into a good mood, regardless.

"Oh, I'm definitely going to be able to go pro after winning this. This was the big one. This was my way in!" Gamma's voice was higher with her excitement, and she sounded genuinely thrilled, more than he had ever heard her in all the time that they had been playing together.

Even Zombie, who rarely seemed to express much excitement seemed to be reveling in this ultimate win for her new squad. "People are going to remember us for sure. We're going to be the biggest names in town."

"Bigger than Slayer?" Blazeman98 asked, is if in an attempt to tease her.

"Way bigger," she responded, without missing a beat.

As much as he wanted to share in their excitement, Cobb couldn't quite muster the same level of enthusiasm. There were so many things that were left unexplained.

"Aren't you guys curious as to what that was all about?"

"I heard someone posted that it was just a special event that got leaked before it was ready," Gamma said. Cobb had seen the same theory floating around, but the explanation just didn't do much to satisfy his curiosity.

"Do you really believe that?" He asked.

"Who cares?" Blaze jumped in. "The whole thing was hardcore, and if that's only part of the event, I can't imagine what the whole thing is going to be like."

"We'll probably be hearing more about it soon, and in the meantime, it's nice to know that we've got a squad together that can handle anything." Gamma pointed out.

The group fell silent for a minute as they all seemed to remember simultaneously that Zombie had never officially joined their squad. Everything had just happened so fast.

"I know you said you prefer playing by yourself, Zombie," Cobbman started when no one else seemed willing to approach the topic. "And now that the storm has passed, I understand if you didn't feel like you need us anymore..."

She jumped in before he had to figure out how to ask her to stay. "But it might be safest to stick around... at least until we know more about what happened."

He was so relieved. "That seems like the best bet."

The tension melted and for the first time since Krypto had left, he found himself in a mood to celebrate by dancing with his entire squad.

No matter what happened, it felt good knowing that they would weather the next storm together.

Made in the USA
Middletown, DE
03 December 2019